PLAY SOCCER

Sheila Fraser

Illustrations by Lisa Kopper

BARRON'S
New York · Toronto

My name's Sean. I want to play soccer.
One day I'm going to be really good.
Dad says it's best to play in the park.
There's a special place for practicing
ball games. We go there a lot.

It's fun running and kicking.
Sometimes I miss altogether.
Sometimes I kick the ball hard
with my foot. Now I've hurt my toe.

"Try to use the side of your foot — your instep,"
says Dad.
"And keep watching
the ball."

I try it but it's not very easy.
Dad says to keep trying.

He puts our sweaters on
the ground and tells me
to kick the ball between
them.

Usually I miss.

Carmel and Jerry play too.
We try kicking the ball
to each other. Sometimes
the ball goes the wrong way.
Carmel thinks that's funny.
She's good at kicking.

I try heading with Dad. We stand close together.
I think it might hurt my head if he throws too hard.
But he says, "Use your forehead, not the top
of your head. Then you won't get a headache."

I did last time.

Next we try to kick balls into a bucket.
Carmel and Jerry can get theirs in the bucket
most of the time. I got mine in once.

Carmel and Jerry are good at juggling the ball too.
They can keep it off the ground for ages.
I drop it a lot. Why does it look so easy
when the famous players do it?

We try to hit the numbers
on the wall. We start
with 1 and try to get to 8.
Even little Jodi thinks
she can do it. I kick the ball
too high. Carmel laughs.

Victoria can see that I feel silly.
It's not fair. Everyone else can do it.
Why can't I?

"Come on, Sean. Cheer up,"
says Dad.
"There's going to be a game.
Nicholas will be goalkeeper."

There are 11 players in World Cup teams. They have to learn lots of rules and practice every day. We haven't got enough people for a World Cup team. Victoria wants to be on my team. There are only five of us.

We start to play. Jerry kicks the ball
to Carmel. Carmel kicks it to me.
And I kick it between the two sweaters.

"Hurray!" screams Carmel. "You scored a goal."
Jerry gives me a hug like real players do.

We start to play again and all the time
I think, "I can do it. I didn't think I could,
but I can. I can play soccer."

What happened to Sean?

Why is Carmel laughing?

How does Jerry practice?